The Wal

Christmas
Stories

Also in this series

The Walker Book of Adventure Stories
The Walker Book of Animal Stories
The Walker Book of Funny Stories
The Walker Book of Magical Stories
The Walker Book of School Stories
The Walker Book of Stunning Stories
The Walker Book of Terrific Tales

This collection published 2001 by Walker Books Ltd
87 Vauxhall Walk, London SE11 5HJ

4 6 8 10 9 7 5 3

Text © year of publication individual authors
Illustrations © year of publication individual illustrators
Cover illustration © 2001 Tony Ross

This book has been typeset in Garamond 3

Printed and bound in Great Britain by Creative Print and Design (Wales), Ebbw Vale

British Library Cataloguing in Publication Data:
a catalogue record for this book is
available from the British Library

ISBN 0-7445-8291-1

www.walkerbooks.co.uk

The Walker Book of Christmas Stories

WALKER BOOKS

AND SUBSIDIARIES

LONDON • BOSTON • SYDNEY • AUCKLAND

Contents

Christmas in Exeter Street

by **DIANA HENDRY**
illustrated by **JOHN LAWRENCE**

The day before Christmas Eve, Ben and Jane's grandma and grandpa came to stay at the house in Exeter Street. It was a lovely old house with big friendly windows, a holly wreath on the front door, and three chimney pots shaped like the crowns of the three wise men.

Grandpa George was a tall old sailor who came in his sea boots. Grandma Ginny came with her knitting and her three cats, One, Two and Three. Wherever Grandma Ginny went, her knitting needles went in and out under her elbows, and One, Two and Three followed along behind her. Grandpa George and Grandma Ginny brought a Christmas tree.

Ben and Jane's mother, Mrs Maggie Mistletoe, showed Grandpa George and Grandma Ginny where they were to sleep. She had given them the best spare bedroom. This had a big four-poster bed in it. Grandpa George parked his sea boots underneath it and the three cats jumped onto the bed and curled up together.

Ben and Jane's other grandma and grandpa also came to the house in Exeter Street. They were small and skinny and wore their best hats, a woolly bobble hat for Grandpa Angus and a beret with stars on it for Grandma Fanny. Grandma Fanny brought a jar of her special cranberry jelly.

Grandpa Angus and Grandma Fanny were given the second-best spare bedroom. This had a small iron bedstead in it. Grandma Fanny said, "This bed is just the right size for two skinnies like us. We can snuggle up together." Grandpa Angus hung his bobble hat on one knob of the bed and Grandma Fanny hung her star-spangled beret on the other knob of the bed.

Ben and Jane's friends – Amelia, Annie and Amos – arrived on Christmas Eve. Their parents had gone to Timbuktu on Very Important Business and so they came to spend Christmas at the house in Exeter Street. Amelia brought a basket of presents, Annie brought a big Christmas pudding and Amos, who was only three, brought his cuddly blanket and it trailed along behind him like a long, long tail.

Mrs Mistletoe took Amelia, Annie and Amos up the stairs to the attic. There they found five beds. Two bunk beds (one for Ben and one for Amos),

two mattresses-on-the-floor (for Jane and Annie) and one camp bed with wobbly legs (for Amelia).

"Mind you all hang up your Christmas stockings," said Mrs Mistletoe.

Amos climbed up and down the ladder to the top bunk, trailing his blankie behind him.

Just after supper an unexpected uncle arrived. It was Uncle Bartholomew back from Australia! Mrs Mistletoe made up a bed for him on the sofa in front of the fire. This was just right for Uncle Bartholomew. Because it had been very hot in Australia he was feeling very chilly; he was so cold he couldn't take off his mittens.

10

Uncle Bartholomew brought a great box of Australian Delight (which was like Turkish Delight, only nicer).

The next to arrive was Mrs Mistletoe's friend Lily, who had nowhere to live. And with Lily came Lily's baby, Lily-Lou. Lily slept on the small sofa in the playroom which had been bounced on so often it was a very funny sagging shape. But this didn't matter because so was Lily. Lily brought home-made Christmas hats, each with a star glued on the front.

The kitchen sink was dried out very carefully, then lined with blankets, and Lily-Lou slept in there. Mrs Mistletoe hung Lily-Lou's stocking over the tap. Lily-Lou brought her smile.

Christmas Eve was very stormy and the vicar's roof blew off, so he and his wife and their four children all came to the house in Exeter Street.

"Is there any room in the inn?" asked the vicar, and Mrs Mistletoe said yes, there was. "We've brought you a carol," said the vicar and they all stood on the doorstep and sang "Away in a Manger".

A bed was made up for the vicar and his wife in the bath and a lot of cushions were piled up in the corridor for the four children.

By this time there was quite a lot of noise in the house in Exeter Street and the children next door – Thomas, Tessa and Timothy – came to join the party. They came in their pyjamas and they brought their sleeping bags and their Christmas stockings and they made a camp in the study.

At nine o'clock five aunts came from Abingdon bringing with them a big turkey and their three Pekinese dogs.

The aunts – Catherine, Clara, Christabel, Clothilda and Christiana – were very thin ladies so each of them was given a shelf on the dresser in the kitchen and tucked up tightly between the plates and the dangling cups.

The Pekinese dogs were packed into shopping

baskets and tucked in with dolls' blankets kindly provided by Jane.

At midnight two fat men knocked at the door and asked for a bed for the night because their car had broken down. Each was given a mantelpiece. The first fat man said, "Please can our wives come in and we will all squash up together on the mantelpiece?"

But the wives were very fat too, and Mrs Mistletoe said she didn't really think two people could fit on one mantelpiece.

"I have two large window-sills to spare," she said. "Would you like to curl up there?" And the wives said yes please and was there a corner for their five children who were still in the car?

Mrs Mistletoe gave a small sigh and said that if Jane and Annie came into her bed, then the five children could sleep on the two mattresses in the attic. The car-children brought an enormous box of crackers.

When everyone was safely tucked up in bed, Mrs Mistletoe counted the number of children asleep in the house in Exeter Street and then she wrote a note for Father Christmas and pinned it on the front door.

Dear Father Christmas,
There are 18 children here.
Please don't forget anyone ~
love,
Maggie Mistletoe
P.S. Lilybou is in the kitchen sink.

No sooner had Mrs Mistletoe got into bed with Jane and Annie than she heard the sound of crying at the front door. She crept down the stairs and looked outside. There on the mat was a small black cat. He brought his snow-white paws. The small black cat slipped inside and found the room where Uncle Bartholomew was asleep on the sofa, dreaming about kangaroos. The small black cat sniffed Uncle Bartholomew and curled up at his feet.

The last person to arrive at the house in Exeter Street had a lot of trouble with his arithmetic. Father Christmas had to take off his boots and count on his toes to make sure he had remembered all eighteen children. And he had. (Even Lily-Lou.)

On Christmas Day morning they took Lily-Lou out of the sink and Mrs Mistletoe and Jane and Grandpa George peeled a whole sack of potatoes and then they all had a splendid Christmas dinner. They ate the Abingdon aunts' turkey with Grandma Fanny's cranberry jelly and afterwards they had Annie's Christmas pudding.

They all wore Lily's Christmas hats (except for Amos who wore his blankie tied round his head because he felt happiest that way) and they pulled the car-children's crackers. When dinner was over they sat round the fire and ate Uncle Bartholomew's Australian Delight and it was like eating sunshine.

Everyone agreed that the house in Exeter Street was the best place of all to be at Christmas time. The little black cat, curled up in Mrs Mistletoe's lap, thought he might stay until next Christmas and Lily-Lou, snuggled up in Uncle Bartholomew's arms, waved her little curly fingers at the Christmas tree and smiled and smiled and smiled.

In Which Tom Appears

by DICK KING-SMITH
illustrated by DAVID PARKINS

Sophie woke early on the morning of her fifth birthday. It was still very dark. Usually the first thing she did when she had switched on the light was to look at the pictures hanging on her bedroom walls. There were four of them, all drawn by Sophie's mother, who was clever at that sort of thing.

One was of a cow called Blossom, one was of two hens named April and May, the third of a Shetland pony called Shorty and the fourth of a spotty pig by the name of Measles.

These were the animals that would one day in the future belong to Sophie, for she was, she said, going to be a lady farmer when she grew up; and neither Sophie's mother and father nor her seven-year-old twin brothers, Matthew and Mark, doubted for one moment that she would.

Sophie, though small, was very determined.

But on this particular morning Sophie did not spare a glance for her portrait gallery. Instead she scrambled to the end of her bed and peered over. And there it was!

"Yikes!" cried Sophie. "He's been!" and she undid the safety-pin that fastened the long bulging woollen stocking to the bedclothes.

By now Sophie was used to the fact that her birthday was on Christmas Day. The twins, who had been born in spring, felt rather sorry for her.

"Poor old Sophie," said Matthew, "being born then."

"Hard luck on her," said Mark. "Glad we weren't."

But Sophie didn't mind.

"It's twice as nice," she said, when anyone asked how she felt about it. "Everybody gives me two presents."

"It was clever of you, Mum," she had said to her mother once.

"What was?"

"Having me on Christmas Day. How did you manage it?"

"With difficulty. But you were the nicest possible Christmas present. Daddy and I both wanted a little girl very much."

"Why?"

"Well, we already had two boys, didn't we?"

"What would you have called me if I'd been a boy?"

"Noël, probably."

"Yuk!" said Sophie. "I'm glad I wasn't, then."

This Christmas Day, the sixth of Sophie's life, started off in the customary way. As soon as the grandmother clock in the hall had struck seven, the twins ran, and Sophie plodded, into their parents' bedroom, and they all climbed onto the big bed to show what Father Christmas had brought them.

Then, after breakfast, came the ceremony of the present-giving.

This was always done in the same way. Everybody sat down, in the sitting-room of course – at least the two grown-ups sat down with their cups of coffee, while Matthew and Mark danced about with excitement, and their sister stood stolidly beside the Christmas tree, beneath which all the presents were arranged, and waited for the

others to sing "Happy birthday, dear Sophie,
happy birthday to you!"

Then the opening of the presents began, one at
a time, youngest first, eldest last – a Christmas

present for Sophie, then one for Mark, then Matthew (ten minutes older), then Mummy, then Dad, and finally a birthday present for Sophie, before she began again on her next Christmas one.

This year, to Sophie's surprise and delight, word of her intention to be a lady farmer had somehow got round the entire family, and both her Christmas and her birthday presents reflected this.

From grandparents and aunts and uncles came picture books of farms and story books of farms and colouring books of farms. Best of all, from her mother and father, there was (for Christmas) a model farmyard with a cowshed and a barn and some post-and-rail fences and a duck pond made of a piece of glass in one corner and (for her birthday) lots of little model animals, cows and sheep and horses, some standing up, some lying down, and a fierce-looking bull, chickens, a turkey-cock, some ducks for the pond, and even a spotty pig.

And as for the present from the twins – that was super, nothing less than a red tractor pulling a yellow trailer!

"The tractor's for your birthday," said Matthew.

"And the trailer's for Christmas," said Mark.

"What a lovely present!" said Sophie's mother.

"Yes," said the twins with one voice. "It was jolly expensive too."

Sophie felt a bit guilty about this, since her Christmas present to them was the usual one –

FARM
MUNNY
THANKYOU
SOPHIE

a Mars bar each, their favourite. Still, that was all she could manage when she had finished buying presents for her parents. Afterwards she had unscrewed the plug in the tummy of her piggy-bank, and found that there was only seven pence of her savings left.

At last there was only one present remaining at the foot of the tree, an ordinary white envelope with SOPHIE written on it. Underneath there was some joined-up writing that Sophie couldn't read. She had left it till last because it looked boring. Probably just an old Christmas card, she thought, as she picked it up and handed it to her father.

"What's it say, Daddy?" she asked.

"It says:

SOPHIE

Many happy returns of Christmas Day
Love from Aunt Al."

Aunt Al was Sophie's Great-great-aunt Alice, who was nearly eighty-one years old and lived in the Highlands of Scotland. She had come to lunch one day in the summer, and she and Sophie had got on like a house on fire.

"Aren't you going to open it?" asked Sophie's mother.

"It's just a card, I expect," said Sophie, but inside the envelope was another smaller envelope marked FARM MONEY and inside that was a five pound note.

"Yikes!" shouted Sophie. "I could buy a hen with that, a real one, I mean!"

"April," said Mark.

"Or May," said Matthew.

"You wait till you get your real farm," said Sophie's father. "This house would be full of animals if you had your way."

After lunch, Sophie set out her model farm on the sitting-room floor. She loaded all the animals in turn onto the trailer, and then drove the tractor into the yard to unload and arrange them.

"You're lucky," she said, holding up the turkey-cock. "We've just been eating one of your lot. Mind you, when I have real turkeys on my farm, I shan't eat any of them."

"You going to be a vegetarian?" asked her mother.

"No," said Sophie, "but you can't eat your friends. I shall eat a stranger – from the supermarket."

"This farm of yours is just going to be a collection of pets," said her father, yawning in his armchair.

"That's right," said Sophie. "I like pets. I wish I had a pet, now."

"You're much too young."

"I'm five."

"That's much too young," said the twins.

"I'll buy myself a pet, with Aunt Al's money."

"Don't be silly," said her father sleepily.

"I'm not silly."

"You are," said Matthew.

"I'm not."

"You are," said Mark.

"I AM NOT."

"Be quiet, Sophie," said her mother, "and play with your toy farm. Daddy wants a nap."

Sophie put the turkey-cock down (on the duck pond, as it happened) and stamped out of the room. Hands rammed deep into the pockets of her jeans, she plodded out into the wintry garden, a short stocky figure whose dark hair looked, as always, as though she had just come through a hedge backwards. Her head was bent, there was a scowl on her round face, and as she walked along the path beside the garden wall, she mouthed the phrase that she always used to describe those who upset her.

"Mowldy, stupid and assive!" she muttered. "That's what they all are, mowldy, stupid and assive. Why can't I have a real live animal of my own – now?"

"Nee-ow?" said a voice above her head, and, looking up, Sophie saw a cat sitting on the wall. It was a jet-black cat with huge round orange eyes that stared down at her, and again it said, more confidently, "Nee-ow!"

Then it jumped down, trotted up to her with its tail held stiffly upright, and began to rub itself against her legs, purring like a steam-engine.

Sophie's frown gave way to a huge grin as she stroked the gleaming sable fur. "Happy Christmas, my dear!" she said. "And how beautiful you are! I wonder who you belong to?"

"Yee-ew!" said the cat.

At least that's how it sounded to Sophie.

The Haunting of Pip Parker

by ANNE FINE
illustrated by
EMMA CHICHESTER CLARK

Maybe you're braver than I am. Maybe it wouldn't spoil your Christmas Eve to have to lie awake feeling haunted, instead of drifting off to sleep knowing you'd wake to find your stocking full of presents.

Maybe you wouldn't mind the night before Christmas being turned into a sort of two-months-late Hallowe'en.

I minded. I minded a lot.

Over there on my desk lay the gifts I'd made, or saved to buy and wrapped up for other people.

Down there at the end of my bed, across my feet, lay my big red (still empty) Christmas stocking.

Above my head hung the glittery Advent calendar I'd made at school, with only one door left to open.

And there, on the far wall, was what was keeping me awake – the horrible tiny golden skull shape that had been shining at me off the wall for a whole week.

Maybe you have stronger nerves than I do. But I couldn't sleep. And I'm not a baby. I managed well enough when I slept over at Great Aunt Belle's, and the branches of her ash tree waved in front of the street light and threw the creepiest shadows you've ever seen over the bedroom wall.

I was fine at Alex's house too, even if it did take me a bit of time to work out that those weird snaky things that kept flitting across the ceiling were just car headlights turning into Mappin Road.

But here in my own home I was a total wreck. I shut my eyes to go to sleep, and had to keep opening them again, to see if the skull was still watching me. Not that it had eyes, exactly. It was just a shape on the wall, a gleaming shape, about the size of my thumb. But it worried me. I couldn't take my eyes off it. And so I couldn't get to sleep, and all week I'd been going around like a zombie, too tired even to think.

And they all kept asking me things – my father, my mother, my elder brother and sister, and Uncle Edward.

"Pip, what do you want for Christmas?"

"Are you short of any winter clothes, darling?"

"Pips, what was the name of that rather nasty plastic thing you saw in the shop window and liked so much?"

"It's Granny on the phone. She wants to know if Pip likes poetry. Do you like poetry, Pip?"

"Simply as a matter of interest, Pip, did you ever find your bike chain?"

I'd try to concentrate. After all, I know as well as you do that it's important to keep your wits about you when people are asking you this sort of question in the last few days before Christmas. Too many wrong answers, and you can fetch up with a pile of junk.

But I was too sleepy to think. And yawning so hard, I couldn't answer anyway.

"Pip! There's only a couple of days left. Please give us a few ideas. What sort of things would you like?"

"Books?"

"Clothes?"

"Pens?"

"Cassettes?"

"Computer stuff?"

Already I was deep in another yawn.

"Pip!"

I made a real effort. But all I wanted for Christmas was to stop being haunted. And that's what I told them.

"All I want for Christmas is for someone to get rid of that horrible thing on my bedroom wall."

"There's nothing on your wall."

"Oh yes, there is!"

"No, there isn't. It's all your imagination. Three times the whole lot of us have trooped upstairs to look for it for you. And every single time there was nothing there."

"It came back as soon as you'd gone."

"Nonsense, Pip."

"Just your imagination."

"Too much cheese."

I can't help it. When I get tired, I get scratchy-tempered. That's just the way I am. I need my sleep. And so, all through last week, when they kept asking me, "Have you decided what you want for Christmas yet?", I kept saying over and over (though I knew how it was annoying them):

"All I want for Christmas is a *nice blank wall*."

You could hear their voices going all frosty. "Right, then. I suppose it will just have to be a surprise."

No one believed me. Nobody offered to come up and have another look. And I could see their point. After all, it was true that they'd been up three times already. Three evenings in a row, when I came down in my pyjamas to complain, they'd all laid their drinks down with a sigh and trooped up the stairs, one after another, moaning.

"I'll tell you Pip's problem. Too much television."

"Have you been eating cheese, dear? Cheese gives you the most vivid dreams."

"Just an excuse to come down again, if you want my opinion."

"Skull on the wall indeed!"

It was there, though. Oh, yes. It was there gleaming at me, as it had been all week. I knew I could go down one last time, but they'd probably get ratty, and might even start teasing me again about the snack Granny had insisted on leaving out "for Santa".

"Who made these little cake things? Was it Pip?"

"They're rock-hard. I can't even sink my teeth into this one."

"A couple of these, and Santa will never get back up the chimney!"

"Did you use flour, Pip? Or Polyfilla?"

No, I was better off up in my bedroom, lying awake staring at the wall and wondering just how the horrible gleaming little skull shape knew exactly when to fold up and disappear.

The last person in the family to come up and have a look was my mother. I heard her hurrying up the stairs and along the landing towards my bedroom, not even stopping to admire the new lamp she'd bought so that Granny could get from the spare room to the bathroom without tripping over the frayed patches in the carpet.

Then she burst through my door.

"Where is it, then?"

And, of course, it had vanished.

"It was here just a moment ago. I was watching it. Honestly."

"Oh, Pip!"

"Just stay a few minutes. Keep absolutely quiet, and see if you can fool it into coming back."

Sighing, she leaned back against the door, and waited.

The seconds passed.

Bored and impatient, she started to drum her fingers behind her on the panels of the door.

"Sssh!" I warned.

She was quiet.

A few more seconds passed. Then: "Pip! I can't stay here all night. Either it's here, or it isn't. And it isn't."

"But it was here. Only a minute ago."

She swung the door open again, and went out.

"I'll shut this behind me," she said. "So the noise from downstairs doesn't keep you awake."

"I'll be awake anyway," I told her. But she'd already gone.

And she was no more than a few steps along the landing before I turned back, and there it was again!

On the wall...

Gleaming at me...

And that's when I did exactly what you would do. I gave up. I gave up trying to have a normal Christmas Eve. I gave up trying to sleep.

I simply lay in bed and waited.

And waited.

And waited.

And waited and waited and waited.

And that's how I came to stay awake longer than anyone else my age, ever, on Christmas Eve. That's how, when I heard the rustling outside, and the rattle of my doorknob, I quickly closed my eyes and pretended as hard as I could that I was fast asleep.

I'm not daft. And I wanted my stocking filled.

I have to tell you, if you didn't know, that Santa's not quite as portly as he looks in most of the pictures you see about. It wasn't easy to tell in the dark, but if you want my opinion he's no fatter than my father. He's no taller either. And he uses much the same language when he stubs his toe against the bedstead.

However, unlike my father, he brought me all I want for Christmas. And this is how.

First, he stepped down to the bottom of my bed. I could hear the rustle of presents being stuffed in my stocking. I thought I'd be safer if I turned my face away. You never know.

I'm sure I'm as good as you are at pretending I'm fast asleep, but you know as well as I do that, once you think someone might be watching you, even in the dark, you get this urge to grin.

So I made a sort of fast-asleep, lip-smacking sound and rolled over restlessly to face the other way.

It was safe to open my eyes now. And there, on the wall, was the gleaming little skull shape.

Behind me, the heavy footsteps went back towards the door.

The skull shape disappeared.

Did I move my foot? I'm sure I didn't move my foot, but it is true that, just at that moment, my Christmas stocking slipped off the bed onto the floor.

The footsteps came back down to the bottom of my bed again.

The skull shape reappeared. I felt a fumbling round my feet.

Then my stocking was laid down on top of them.

The footsteps went back to the door. The shape on the wall vanished.

I moved my foot – only a tiny bit. I didn't mean to tip the stocking onto the floor again.

I won't tell you what Santa muttered. You wouldn't want to know, and, if you did, your family wouldn't want you to repeat it.

The footsteps came back down to the end of the bed.

The skull shape reappeared. The stocking landed on the bed again. (Quite hard.)

The footsteps went back to the door. The skull shape vanished.

And suddenly, instantly, in a flash, I had all I wanted for Christmas! And I don't mean a stocking full of presents.

No! I didn't care if what was crushing my feet was wonderful presents I'd longed for all my life, or just some old heap of bike chains and poetry books and winter clothes. (To be perfectly honest with you, even now I haven't bothered to pull them out of the stocking and unwrap them.)

No. All I did was slip out of bed, pad over to the door in my bare feet, and stuff that stupid skull-shaped keyhole so full of torn up scraps of wrapping paper that no light would ever again be able to shine through from the other side and make gleaming shapes on my wall.

Maybe you're brighter than I am. Maybe you would have cottoned on the very first evening, and

known straight away that the new lamp on the landing was to blame.

Maybe you would have realized at once that the reason nobody else could ever see the skull shape on the wall was because they were leaning against the door and blocking the light through the keyhole. Maybe.

Well, you may be brighter than I am, but you couldn't be more tired. I'm going off to sleep now – my first good sleep for a week. Oh, I know the whole lot of them will be at me again in the morning.

"Where's Pip?"

"Still not up? Really! On Christmas Day!"

"Someone yell upstairs, quickly."

"Pip! Pip! We're waiting for you! Hurry up!"

It won't do them any good. I won't even be awake to hear. They can go ahead and open their presents without me. I have all I want for Christmas already – a nice blank wall. And that means a good, long, deep and dreamless sleep. I'm starting it right now.

And I shan't give my best present up that easily.

Neither would you.

Caroline's Christmas

by MICK GOWAR
illustrated by DUNCAN SMITH

It was the afternoon of Christmas Eve, and Caroline was almost bursting with excitement and frustration. So many wonderful things were *going* to happen – but not yet.

Under the Christmas tree a huge mound of presents was waiting to be opened; upstairs, on Caroline's bed, her empty stocking was waiting to be hung up (and filled with presents). Caroline was waiting, too, for Granny and Grandad. That was the first exciting thing that was going to happen: Granny and Grandad were coming to stay for Christmas. They were due to arrive at three o'clock.

Caroline looked at her watch again. It seemed like hours since lunch. It must be three o'clock now, thought Caroline. She concentrated on the hands of her watch, trying to work out the time, but it was very difficult. One of Mickey Mouse's hands was pointing to the one, so that it meant it was five past something; but the other hand wasn't pointing directly at a number – it was halfway between the three and the four. It was either five past three or five past four, but whichever it was, Granny and Grandad were late.

"Mum, what's the time?"

"For goodness sake, Caroline," Mum called back from the kitchen, "it's only five minutes later than the last time you asked me. It's almost twenty past one."

Mum came into the living room wiping her hands on her striped apron. "They won't be here for hours. Why don't you play a game?"

"I can't think of any games."

"What about Snakes and Ladders…?" suggested Mum.

"I can't play Snakes and Ladders on my own," Caroline interrupted.

"Well then, how about a jigsaw?" Mum continued. "You like jigsaws."

"No I don't," replied Caroline, crossly. "Jigsaws are boring."

"I know, you can draw a nice picture to give to Granny and Grandad when they arrive. They'd love that."

"I can't think of anything to draw."

"You can draw the Christmas tree and all the presents – that's a great idea. Here –" and before Caroline could object, Mum handed her a pad of paper and her tin of felt-tip pens. "And Caroline, please – no questions for a while. I must finish stuffing the turkey before they arrive."

Mum went back to the kitchen, and Caroline settled down on the floor, a few feet from the tree. She gazed at the pile of presents. The tiny fairy lights on the tree made the shiny wrapping paper glitter and sparkle; the brightly coloured faces of Father Christmas and Rudolf the Red-nosed Reindeer twinkled and their eyes seemed to wink mischievously at Caroline.

"Shake me…" they seemed to be saying, "squeeze me … open me!"

Caroline moved a little closer to the tree. Slowly, she stretched out a hand to touch the nearest present. It was long and tube-shaped, and it had been wrapped to look like a cracker. Caroline gave it a tiny squeeze.

Whatever was in the parcel flattened slightly, and then sprang back into shape.

It must be one of those squeaky squeezy toys, thought Caroline, rather disappointed. She gave it another squeeze, to see what sort of noise it made – *gloop*, went the toy.

It didn't sound right. Luckily, one end of the parcel wasn't properly stuck down. Caroline pushed one finger into the top and wiggled it about. She felt something like a bottle-top turning. She gave it another twist. Yes, it was definitely turning.

Caroline removed her finger and tried to peer into the open end of the parcel. As she did so, she gave the present another hard squeeze. Without warning, a jet of thick liquid shot out into her face.

"Ow!" she screamed. "Ooooh! Owww!" The thick smelly liquid was stinging her eyes.

Caroline's cries brought Mum rushing from the kitchen.

"Caroline! What on earth do you think you're doing?"

"Help!" shrieked Caroline. "It's in my eyes! I can't see! Ooooh! Owwwwww!"

"Serves you right," snapped Mum, as she bathed Caroline's eyes with cold water. "That was Granny's special bath oil. It was a very naughty thing to do. You can go and sit in your room until Granny and Grandad get here; and I don't want to hear another peep out of you until they arrive!"

*"...But I heard him exclaim as he drove out of sight,
'Happy Christmas to all, and to all a good night.'"*

Grandad closed the pages of the special Christmas book, and Caroline snuggled down into bed. One by one, Granny, Grandad, Mum and Dad kissed her goodnight and tiptoed downstairs.

It had been a lovely afternoon. Granny had brought her an enormous bag of jelly babies ("Just to be going on with"). Grandad had given her a pound coin ("And don't tell your mum!"). And at tea, when Caroline had whined for a piece of Christmas cake and Mum had said it was for tomorrow, Granny had said, "Oh go on, let her – it *is* Christmas after all."

Caroline closed her eyes and tried to will herself to sleep. She knew the sooner she was asleep, the sooner it would be morning and the sooner she could open her presents.

She hugged her special rabbit toy, Bugs, a little tighter. The thought of all the presents under the tree, and Father Christmas and her stocking … it was all *so* exciting! Caroline sat up to check that her stocking was still hanging on the end of the bed and hadn't slipped off. It was still there. Good.

Caroline lay down on her tummy again, but she couldn't settle. She tried lying on her left side, but that was no better. She tried her right, still not comfortable.

Caroline lay on her back and stared at the ceiling. From downstairs, she could hear the sounds of the TV (it was louder than usual because of Granny's bad ear). She could hear Mum, Dad, Granny and Grandad laughing. Softly, she started to recite the names of Father Christmas's reindeer from the story Grandad had read: "Dasher, Dancer, Prancer, Vixen … erm … Something, Someone, Donner, Blitzen—"

Reindeer! Caroline sat up with a start. She'd forgotten the reindeer! After tea, she'd put a mince pie and a glass of whisky on the back doorstep for Father Christmas, but she hadn't left anything for the reindeer! What if Father Christmas didn't leave presents for people who forgot his reindeer?

She jumped out of bed and tiptoed downstairs. The TV set was blaring so loudly no one heard her creep along the hall and into the kitchen.

Caroline switched on the light and looked hopefully around for something that reindeer might like to eat. There was the Christmas cake, still on the table. Did reindeer like Christmas cake? Caroline decided they probably didn't. She opened the larder door. Chocolate biscuits? No. Christmas pudding? No again. Pickled onions? Definitely not!

She was just closing the larder door when she saw a large pan of peeled sprouts on the floor. That would have to do. Hay would be better, she thought, but at least sprouts came from plants. Sprouts were better than nothing.

Caroline picked up the pan. It was much heavier than it looked. She began to stagger towards the back door, slopping water as she went. She was still a long way from the door when she felt the heavy pan begin to slip from her grasp.

Crash! The metal pan hit the tiled floor, and a tidal wave of sprouts and cold water swept across the kitchen.

Mum, Dad, Granny and Grandad all came running to see what had happened.

"Caroline!" yelled Dad. "What on earth are you doing?"

"It was … it was … for the reindeer…" Caroline stammered.

"Oh no it wasn't!" snapped Dad. "That was for *our* Christmas dinner. Now I'm going to have to pick them all up, and wash the kitchen floor again. I think you'd better go back to bed, before I lose my temper!"

Caroline awoke with a start. It was dark, and very late. The hall light had been switched off.

She sat up. She could see by the soft glow of her night-light that her stocking was still dangling empty on the end of her bed.

Then she heard the sound of someone tiptoeing rather noisily along the landing. She knew from the sound of the footsteps that it wasn't Mum or Dad, so it must be – *him*!

Quivering with excitement, Caroline crept to her bedroom door and peeped out. There was no one on the top landing, but the bathroom light was on. From the bathroom Caroline could hear a deep male voice softly humming "Jingle Bells".

He's washing his hands, she thought. He must get ever so dirty climbing up and down chimneys.

The bathroom light went off. A few seconds later, Caroline saw the dark outline of a tall tubby figure leave the bathroom and begin creeping back along the landing. She could see that he was wearing what looked like a large cloak and, as he reached the top of the stairs, she couldn't restrain herself any longer.

"Father Christmas!" she shrieked.

There was a crash, a splash and the sound of something small and hard bouncing down the stairs.

"Who the blazes is that?" shouted the startled figure. He fumbled in the darkness. The light went on, and there stood Grandad, dressed in his dressing gown and slippers. At his feet lay a broken glass and a pool of water and, halfway down the stairs, a pair of gleaming false teeth.

Caroline turned round, and saw her parents glaring down at her.

"Go to bed – now!" snapped Dad. "And go to *sleep*!"

The next time Caroline woke up it was really and truly Christmas morning. Her stocking was bulging, and Mickey's long arm was pointing at the seven and his other hand was between the five and the six.

"Mum! Dad! He's come! He's come!" Caroline yelled, as she ran into her parents' bedroom, dragging her stocking behind her.

"Ogggfh!" said Dad. "Wassertime?"

He switched on the bedside light and tried to focus on the clock with one bloodshot eye.

"It's twenty-five past seven," said Caroline proudly, showing him Mickey.

Dad groaned.

Caroline climbed over him, snuggled down between Mum and Dad, and started to unpack her stocking.

"Happy Christmas, darling," said Mum, without opening her eyes. "John ... is it very early?"

Dad groaned again. "Well, Caroline reckons it's nearly half past seven. I'd say ... oooh, approximately twenty to six—"

"Mum! Dad! Look what I've got!" Caroline squealed with delight. "It's just what I wanted – a toy trumpet! Listen, I'll play you a tune. What would you like to hear?"

"How about 'Silent Night'," suggested Mum.

"That's quite a hard one," said Caroline, frowning. "But I'll do my best. Here goes..."

The Boot Gang's Christmas Caper

by SARAH HAYES
illustrated by JUAN WIJNGAARD

Annie Boot was a burglar. Her father had been a burglar, and so had her grandfather. And when Annie Boot had twin boys, they turned out to be burglars too.

When he was little, Jojo Boot was good at climbing trees and balancing on washing lines. Annie hoped that he might grow up to be a big star in the circus. But Jojo became a burglar instead.

Bubbles Boot loved to take apart old clocks and radios, and he was very clever at making working models out of bits and pieces. Annie thought that Bubbles might grow up to be an engineer, or even an inventor. But Bubbles became a burglar like his brother.

The Boots were well known to the police, and they were on Wanted posters all over town. But the Boot Gang had never been caught: the fact is that Annie Boot was a master of disguise. No one ever recognized her or Jojo or Bubbles, not on the beach, nor in the theatre, nor at the museum, nor at football matches or garden fêtes or civic parades.

But everyone knew when the Boot Gang had been at work.

Of all their disguises, Annie's favourite was the one they used only once a year, for the great Christmas Caper. The false beard made Annie sneeze and Jojo found the sledge heavy going. Bubbles complained about always having to be the back end. But as a disguise it worked beautifully.

If people looked out of their windows and saw a reindeer waiting patiently under the lamplight, they smiled to themselves and drew their curtains.

If children woke in the night to find a person in

red beside their beds, they quickly closed their eyes and turned over.

If there seemed to be odd thuds on the roof and sneezings in the chimney, no one paid attention – not on Christmas Eve.

Every year Annie and Jojo and Bubbles stole presents from under trees, from bottom drawers and the tops of wardrobes, and even out of stockings and pillowcases.

When they got home, the Boots made three huge piles of presents and unwrapped them. Jojo and Bubbles didn't always get what they wanted, but Annie was always delighted.

"That'll come in handy," she'd say, and it always did. Of course, the Boots didn't bother giving each other presents, but nobody minded that.

Eventually the Boot Gang became so rich that they decided to give up burgling and retire.

"We could lie on the beach sometimes," said Jojo. "I could learn to swim."

"We could go to the opera," said Annie.

"And drive out to the country," said Bubbles.

"There will be one last Christmas Caper," said Annie, "and it will be the best ever."

The Boot Gang set to work at once. Bubbles designed a power-assisted sledge. Jojo taught Annie to walk along roof ridges and come down

chimneys without making a sound. Annie created an improved reindeer costume that didn't sag in the middle and had a truly magnificent set of antlers. And she made herself a new false beard that didn't tickle her nose and make her sneeze.

The Boots studied maps and made elaborate plans. They practised split-second timing with Annie's stopwatches. Jojo and Bubbles put on their reindeer costume and taught themselves to trot and gallop and even to jump over small obstacles. It was going to be the best Christmas Caper ever, and nothing could possibly go wrong.

Annie usually picked parts of the town where rich people lived, because they had the biggest, most expensive presents. This year she chose Willow Walk, because that was where the richest people of all lived.

On Christmas Eve the weather was perfect. The snow had stopped, and there was just enough moon to light up the roof-tops.

"Look at all those stars," said Bubbles, but Annie told him to be quiet and get into the back of the reindeer.

All went exactly as they had planned. The runners of the new, power-assisted sledge slid smoothly along the snow-covered roads, and the improved reindeer trotted elegantly in front, lifting its feet and pointing its hooves. No one heard sneezings in the chimneys of Willow Walk. And only a sprinkling of soot dropped into the grates as Annie slipped into house after house and left with her sack by way of the front door.

At the end of Willow Walk stood a funny little house quite different from the rest. Annie didn't remember ever having seen it before. She decided not to bother with it. Then Jojo looked through the window and gasped.

"Look at that!" he whispered to Bubbles.

"Look at what?" said Bubbles crossly. He couldn't see anything from the back end of the reindeer.

Just then Annie came out of the house next door. She looked through the window of the funny little house and gasped, just like Jojo. There was the

tallest Christmas tree and the biggest pile of presents Annie had ever seen in her life.

"We've got to have some of those," said Jojo, and Annie agreed.

The chimney of the funny little house was narrow and dirty, and Annie got covered in soot. But she soon found the room with the tall Christmas tree and the enormous pile of presents. She had almost filled her sack when she heard a cough behind her.

"Ho-ho-ho," said Annie gruffly, which was what she usually said if anyone saw her.

"And a ho-ho-ho to you," said someone in a very deep voice.

Annie started. This wasn't what usually happened, not at all. She turned round, gave a little scream, and dropped her sack. Standing in front of her was a person in red with a huge white beard and big black boots; someone who looked very like Annie herself.

"You're not..." quavered Annie. "You're not the real..." Annie's voice trailed off into silence.

"Ho-ho-ho," the person in red said again.

Annie pulled herself together. She strode across the room and gave a tug on the huge white beard.

"Ouch!" said the person in red.

Then Annie did something she had never done before. She fainted dead away.

"That's what comes of taking other people's presents, Annie Boot," said Father Christmas. He picked Annie off the floor and put her gently down in a soft armchair. Then he shouldered his sack and vanished up the chimney.

In the street outside Jojo and Bubbles were also in trouble. One minute Jojo was half asleep and dreaming about the huge pile of presents. And the next, something started to woofle at him. Then something else stamped on his foot. Jojo opened his eyes and shut them again very quickly. Crowding curiously around him and Bubbles, and all woofling and stamping in the cold air, were eight enormous reindeer.

Jojo panicked. He put down his antlers and tried to charge off at full gallop. Bubbles had no idea what was happening and he tried to trot elegantly. As a result the twins got absolutely nowhere and fell in a tangled heap on the snow. The two halves of the reindeer came apart with a horrible tearing sound.

Out of the darkness above the roof-tops came a

long, low whistle. The eight reindeer pricked up their ears, and with a great whooshing noise, they took off into the air and disappeared.

Two policemen coming round the corner of Willow Walk heard the whistle.

"Something's going on," said one of the policemen. They hurried towards the noise and ran straight into the heap of struggling Boots.

"It's our lucky night," said the policemen as they marched the Boot Gang towards the police station. Annie and Jojo and Bubbles said nothing. They looked white and very shaken.

The Boot Gang spent Christmas in prison that year, and the next, and several more after that. They never spoke about what had happened on the last Christmas Caper.

Eventually the time came for the Boots to leave prison. They were going to be released on New Year's Day, and they could hardly wait for Christmas to be over. On Christmas morning, however, Jojo woke up to find a present on the end of his bunk. "For Jojo Boot," said the label.

"I've never had a present specially for me," shouted Jojo. "Who sent it?" But no one seemed to know. Annie and Bubbles had presents on their beds too.

Jojo tore open the wrappings, and found a pair of waterwings, some sunglasses and a shirt with palm trees on it. Bubbles had a set of spanners and a pair of bright blue overalls. Annie had a ticket for the opera and some very sharp cutting shears.

And when they came out of prison the Boot Gang stopped being burglars. Jojo learned to swim and became a lifeguard. Bubbles joined a garage that repaired old sports cars. And Annie got a job making costumes for the theatre. They were very busy and very happy. Every Christmas the Boots gave each other presents, and they always got exactly what they wanted.

One day, quite by chance, Annie found herself in Willow Walk. She hurried past all the grand houses, glancing occasionally to left and right.

It was a curious thing, but she just couldn't seem to find the funny little house at the end of the row. Just as well, Annie thought, and she caught the bus back to work.

The Boots never found out who had sent them the mysterious presents in prison. But once in a while Jojo or Bubbles would hear a long, low whistle above the roof-tops on Christmas Eve. And Annie would think back to the very last Christmas Caper. "Never again," she would say, and shake her head. And sometimes, very, very occasionally, she would catch the faint sound of a "ho-ho-ho" in the chimney.

The Christmas Miracle of Jonathan Toomey

by SUSAN WOJCIECHOWSKI
illustrated by P.J. LYNCH

The village children called him Mr Gloomy.

But, in fact, his name was Toomey, Mr Jonathan Toomey. And though it's not kind to call people names, this one fitted quite well. For Jonathan Toomey seldom smiled and never laughed. He went about mumbling and grumbling, muttering and sputtering, grumping and griping. He complained that the church bells rang too often, that the birds sang too shrilly, that the children played too loudly.

Mr Toomey was a wood-carver. Some said he was the best wood-carver in the whole valley. He spent his days sitting at a workbench, carving beautiful shapes from blocks of pine and hickory and chestnut wood. After supper, he sat in a straight-backed chair near the fireplace, smoking his pipe and staring into the flames.

Jonathan Toomey wasn't an old man, but if you saw him, you might think he was, the way he walked bent forwards with his head down. You wouldn't notice his eyes, the clear blue of an August sky. And you wouldn't see the dimple on his chin, since his face was mostly hidden under a shaggy, untrimmed beard, speckled with sawdust and wood shavings and, depending on what he'd eaten that day, crumbs of bread or a bit of potato or dried gravy.

The village people didn't know it, but there was a reason for his gloom, a reason for his grumbling, a reason why he walked hunched over, as if carrying a great weight on his shoulders. Some years earlier, when Jonathan Toomey was young and full of life and full of love, his wife and baby had become very ill. And, because those were the days before hospitals and medicines and skilled doctors, his wife and baby had died, three days apart from each other.

So Jonathan Toomey had packed his belongings into a wagon and travelled till his tears stopped. He settled into a tiny house at the edge of a village to do his wood-carving.

One day in early December, there was a knock at Jonathan's door. Mumbling and grumbling, he went to answer it. There stood a woman and a young boy.

"I'm the widow McDowell. I'm new to your village. This is my son, Thomas," the woman said.

"I'm seven and I know how to whistle," said Thomas.

"Whistling is pish-posh," said the wood-carver gruffly.

"I need something carved," said the woman and she told Jonathan about a very special set of Christmas figures her grandfather had carved for her when she was a girl.

"After I moved here, I discovered that they were lost," she explained. "I had hoped that by some miracle I would find them again, but it hasn't happened."

"There are no such things as miracles," the wood-carver told her. "Now, could you describe the figures for me?"

"There were sheep," she told him.

"Two of them, with curly wool," added Thomas.

"Yes, two," said the widow, "and a cow, an angel, Mary, Joseph, the Baby Jesus, and the Wise Men."

"Three of them," added Thomas.

"Will you take the job?" asked the widow McDowell.

"I will."

"I'm grateful. How soon can you have them ready?"

"They will be ready when they are ready," he said.

"But I must have them by Christmas. They mean very much to me. I can't remember a Christmas without them."

"Christmas is pish-posh," said Jonathan gruffly and he shut the door.

The following week there was a knock at the wood-carver's door. Muttering and sputtering, he went to answer it. There stood the widow McDowell and Thomas.

"Excuse me," said the widow, "but Thomas has been begging to come and watch you work. He says he wants to be a wood-carver when he grows up and would like to watch you since you are the best in the valley."

"I'll be quiet. You won't even know I'm here. Please, please," piped in Thomas.

With a grumble, the wood-carver stepped aside to let them in. He pointed to a stool near his workbench. "No talking, no jiggling, no noise," he ordered Thomas.

The widow McDowell handed Mr Toomey a

warm loaf of corn bread as a token of thanks. Then she took out her knitting and sat down in a rocking-chair in the far corner of the cottage.

"Not there!" bellowed the wood-carver. "No one sits in that chair." So she moved to the straight-backed chair by the fire.

Thomas sat very still. Once, when he needed to sneeze, he pressed a finger under his nose to hold it back. Once, when he wanted desperately to scratch his leg, he counted to twenty to keep his mind off the itch.

After a very long time, Thomas cleared his throat and whispered, "Mr Toomey, may I ask a question?"

The wood-carver glared at Thomas, then shrugged his shoulders and grunted. Thomas decided it meant "yes", so he went on. "Is that my sheep you're carving?"

The wood-carver nodded and grunted again.

After another very long time, Thomas whispered, "Mr Toomey, excuse me, but you're carving my sheep wrong."

The widow McDowell's knitting-needles stopped clicking. Jonathan Toomey's knife stopped carving. Thomas went on. "It's a beautiful sheep, nice and curly, but my sheep looked happy."

"That's pish-posh," said Mr Toomey. "Sheep are sheep. They cannot look happy."

"Mine did," answered Thomas. "They knew they were with the Baby Jesus, so they were happy."

After that, Thomas was quiet for the rest of the afternoon. When the church bells chimed six o'clock, Mr Toomey grumbled under his breath about the awful noise. The widow McDowell said it was time to leave. Thomas sneezed three times, then thanked the wood-carver for allowing him to watch.

That evening, after a supper of corn bread and boiled potatoes, the wood-carver sat down at his bench. He picked up his knife. He picked up the sheep. He worked until his eyelids drooped shut.

A few days later there was a knock at the wood-carver's door. Griping and grumbling, he went to answer it. There stood the widow and her son.

"May I watch again? I will be quiet," said Thomas.

He settled himself on the stool very quietly, while his mother laid a basket of sweet-smelling raisin buns on the table.

"The teapot is warm," Mr Toomey said gruffly, his head bent over his work.

While Mr Toomey carved, the widow McDowell poured tea. She touched the wood-carver gently on the shoulder and placed a cup of tea and a bun next to him. He pretended not to notice, but soon, both the plate and the cup were empty.

Thomas tried to eat the bun his mother had given him as quietly as he could. But it is almost impossible to be seven and eat a warm sticky raisin bun without making various smacking, licking, satisfied noises.

When Thomas had finished, he tried to sit quietly. Once, he almost hiccuped, but he took a deep breath and held it till his face turned red. And once, without thinking, he began to swing his legs, but a glare from the wood-carver stopped him and he kept them so still they fell asleep.

After a very long time, Thomas whispered, "Mr Toomey, excuse me, may I ask a question?"

Grunt.

"Is that my cow you're carving?"

Nod and grunt.

Another very long time went by. Then Thomas cleared his throat and said, "Mr Toomey, excuse me, but I must tell you something. That is a beautiful cow, the most beautiful cow I have ever seen, but it's not right. My cow looked proud."

"That's pish-posh," growled the wood-carver. "Cows are cows. They cannot look proud."

"My cow did. It knew that Jesus chose to be born in its barn, so it was proud."

Thomas was quiet for the rest of the afternoon. The only sounds that could be heard were the scraping of the carving knife, the humming of the widow McDowell and the *click-click* of her knitting-needles.

When the church bells chimed six o'clock, Mr Toomey muttered under his breath about the noise. The widow McDowell said it was time to leave. Thomas shook first one leg, then the other. He thanked the wood-carver for allowing him to watch.

That evening, after a supper of boiled potatoes and raisin buns, the wood-carver sat down at his bench. He picked up his carving knife. He picked up the cow. He worked until his eyelids drooped shut.

A few days later there was a knock on the wood-carver's door. He smoothed down his hair as he went to answer it. At the door were the widow and her son.

"May I watch again?" asked Thomas.

As Mrs McDowell warmed the tea and put a plate of fresh molasses biscuits on the workbench, Thomas watched the wood-carver work on the figure of an angel.

After a very long time, Thomas spoke. "Mr Toomey, excuse me, is that my angel you're carving?"

"Yes. And would you do me the favour of telling me exactly what I'm doing wrong?"

"Well, my angel looked like one of God's most important angels, because it was sent to Baby Jesus."

"And just how does one make an angel look important?" asked the wood-carver.

"You'll be able to do it," said Thomas. "You are the best wood-carver in the valley."

After another very long time, Thomas spoke. "Mr Toomey, excuse me, may I ask a question?"

"Do you ever stop talking?" asked the wood-carver.

"My mother says I don't. She says I could learn about the virtue of silence from you."

Under his beard, the wood-carver's face turned pink. The widow McDowell's face turned as red as the scarf she was knitting.

"Well, speak up, what is your question?"

"Will you please teach me to carve?"

"I am a very busy man," grumbled the wood-carver. But he put down the important angel. "You will carve a bird."

"A robin, I hope," said Thomas. "I like robins."

With a piece of charcoal, the wood-carver sketched a robin on a piece of brown paper. He handed Thomas a small block of pine and a knife. He showed him how to lop the corners from the block and slowly smooth the edges of the wood into curves.

Thomas copied the wood-carver's strokes, head bent, tongue working from side to side of his lower lip as he concentrated.

When the church bells chimed six o'clock, Jonathan Toomey was holding Thomas's hand in his, guiding the knife along the edge of a wing. He didn't hear them ringing. The widow McDowell said it was time to leave. Thomas brushed wood shavings from his shirt. Then he reached out and brushed two especially large pieces of wood shaving from Jonathan Toomey's beard. He thanked the wood-carver for teaching him how to carve.

Later, after a supper of boiled potatoes and molasses biscuits, Jonathan Toomey went to his workbench. He thought for a long time. He sketched drawing after drawing. Finally, he picked up his carving knife. He picked up the angel. He carved until his eyelids drooped shut.

A few days later, there was a knock on the

woodcarver's door. Mr Toomey jumped up to answer it.

There stood the widow McDowell with a bouquet of pine branches and holly sprigs, dotted with berries. And there stood Thomas, clutching his partly-carved robin.

While Thomas and Mr Toomey carved, Mrs McDowell put the branches in a jar of water. She scrubbed Mr Toomey's kitchen table and set the jar in the centre, on a pretty cloth embroidered with lilies of the valley and daisies which she found in a drawer below the cupboard.

"Next, I will carve the Wise Men and Joseph," the wood-carver said to Thomas. "Perhaps, before I begin, you will tell me about all the mistakes I am going to make."

"Well," said Thomas, "my Wise Men were wearing their most wonderful robes because they were going to visit Jesus, and my Joseph was leaning over Baby Jesus like he was protecting him. He looked very serious."

It wasn't until the church bells had chimed and the widow and her son were preparing to go that Mr Toomey saw the jar of pine branches and the scrubbed table and the cloth embroidered with lilies of the valley and daisies.

"I found the cloth in a drawer. I thought it would look pretty on the table," the widow McDowell said, smiling.

"Never open that drawer," the wood-carver said harshly.

When the two had left, Jonathan put the cloth away.

That evening, after a supper of boiled potatoes, the wood-carver worked on Joseph and the Wise Men until his eyelids drooped shut.

A few days later there was a knock on the woodcarver's door. He dusted the crumbs from his beard and brushed the sawdust from his shirt. At the door were the widow McDowell and Thomas.

All afternoon Thomas watched the wood-carver work. When it was time to leave, Jonathan said to Thomas, "I am about to begin the last two figures – Mary and the baby. Can you tell me how your figures looked?"

"They were the most special of all," said Thomas. "Jesus was smiling and reaching up to his mother and Mary looked like she loved him very much."

"Thank you, Thomas," said the wood-carver.

"Tomorrow is Christmas. Is there any chance the

figures will be ready?" the widow McDowell asked.

"They will be ready when they are ready."

"I understand," said the widow, and she handed Jonathan two parcels. "Merry Christmas," she said.

Jonathan folded his arms across his chest. "I want no presents," he said harshly.

"That is exactly why we are giving them," answered the widow. She put them down on the table and left.

Jonathan sat down at the table. Slowly, he opened the first parcel. Inside was a red scarf, hand-knitted, warm and bright. He tied the scarf around his neck.

The other parcel held a robin, crudely carved of pine. A smile twitched at the corners of Jonathan's mouth as he ran his fingers over the lopsided wings. He dusted the mantelpiece with his sleeve and placed the robin exactly in the centre, so he could look at it from his chair.

The wood-carver did not eat supper that day. Instead he began to sketch the final figures, Mary and Jesus. He drew Mary, then crumpled the sketch into a ball and tossed it on the floor. He drew the baby, crumpled the sketch into a ball and tossed it with the first. He sketched again. Once more he crumpled the paper. Soon there was a small mountain of crumpled papers at his feet. He picked up a block of wood and tried to carve, but his knife would not do what he wanted it to do. He hurled the chunk of wood into the fireplace and sat, staring into the flames.

When he heard the church bells announcing the midnight Christmas service, he got up. Slowly he opened the drawer beneath the cupboard, the drawer he had told the widow never to open.

From it he took the cloth embroidered with lilies of the valley and daisies. He took out a rough woollen shawl and a lace handkerchief. He took out a tiny white baby blanket and a little pair of blue socks. He placed each piece gently on the floor. From the bottom of the drawer he lifted out a picture frame, beautifully carved of deep brown chestnut wood.

In the frame was a charcoal sketch of a woman sitting in a rocking-chair, holding a baby. The baby's arms were reaching up, touching the woman's face. The woman was looking down at the baby, smiling. Jonathan sat down in his rocking-chair and held the picture against his chest. He rocked slowly, his eyes closed. Two tears trailed into his beard.

When he finally took the picture to his workbench and began to carve, his fingers worked quickly and surely. He carved all through the night.

The next day, there was a knock on the widow McDowell's door.

When she opened it, there stood the woodcarver, his neck wrapped in a red scarf, holding a wooden box stuffed with straw.

"Mr Toomey!" said the widow. "What a surprise. Merry Christmas."

"The figures are ready," he said as he stepped inside.

From the box, Jonathan unpacked two curly sheep, happy sheep because they were with Jesus. He unpacked a proud cow and an angel, a very important angel with mighty wings stretching from its shoulders right down to the hem of its gown. He unpacked three Wise Men wearing their most wonderful robes, edged with fur and falling in rich folds.

He unpacked a serious and caring Joseph. He unpacked Mary wearing a rough woollen shawl, looking down, loving her precious baby son. Jesus was smiling and reaching up to touch his mother's face.

That day, Jonathan went to the Christmas service with the widow McDowell and Thomas. And that day in the churchyard the village children saw Jonathan throw back his head, showing his eyes as clear as an August sky, and laugh. No one ever called him Mr Gloomy again.

Sarah's Christmas

by **MARTIN WADDELL**
illustrated by **PATRICK BENSON**

It was Christmas Day!

Sarah woke up and there, at the end of her bed, was her stocking.

"Ooooooh!" she said, and she bounced down her bed and grabbed it.

There were new mittens inside, and a scarf, and an orange, and some chocolate money, and a book about kittens and a flute.

Sarah blew the flute and wakened her little baby sister, Maeve. Maeve only had a tiny stocking, because she was a tiny baby.

There were sweeties in it, and a doll, and mittens.

"Just like mine!" said Sarah.

"Mine!" said Maeve, bouncing up and down in her cot. All the bouncing and flute playing made so much noise that Sarah's dad had to come up and see what was happening.

"Oh, look!" said Sarah, suddenly.

There was a trail of golden dust leading from the end of Sarah's bed, where her stocking had been, to the end of Maeve's cot, where her stocking had been, and onto the bedroom chair, where somebody had been sitting. You could tell that somebody had been sitting there, because the chair was covered in golden dust, and the same somebody had eaten the biscuits that Sarah had left for him, and finished the orange juice!

"Santa Claus!" gasped Sarah, touching the golden dust, which made her hand golden too.

"He must have come down the chimney!" said Sarah's dad.

"Don't be silly," said Sarah. "We haven't got a chimney!"

Sarah's mum helped Sarah to follow the trail of gold right round the room and out of the door, where it stopped on the landing.

"Where did he go to?" asked Sarah's mum.

"The roof-space!" said Sarah. "He came through the trapdoor."

"You're *probably* right," said Dad.

"But how did he get *into* the roof-space?" asked Sarah.

Sarah's dad looked at Sarah's mum, and Sarah's mum looked at Sarah's dad, and he shrugged. "Don't know, Sarah!" he said.

"Maybe there's a hole in the roof," said Sarah.

"I expect that's it," said Mum.

"Presents time, I think!" said Dad.

Sarah got a big doll, much bigger than the little one in Maeve's stocking, and a book called *Famous Fairy Tales* and sweeties and two jigsaw puzzles and a pair of skates and a crash helmet.

Maeve got a new hat, and a coat, and three pairs of red tights, and sweeties, and a pull-along jingle dog, and a musical clock.

Sarah started playing with the clock.

"Mine!" said Maeve, crawling towards it.

"I was only playing with it," said Sarah, putting it behind her back where Maeve couldn't get at it.

"Children!" said Mum. "Remember, it is Christmas."

"Peace!" said Dad. "Everybody has to be good and kind and nice to each other on Christmas Day."

"I know," said Sarah, letting go of the clock. "Fred told me."

"Fred?" said Dad.

"He's Sarah's Angel," said Mum. "Sarah can see him in the garden. He jumps off trees!"

"He can fly now," said Sarah. "He's passed his Wings Test!"

"Oh," said Dad. "Well done, Fred, wherever you are!"

"He's in Heaven, of course!" said Sarah, who thought her dad was being really silly. Everyone knows Angels live in Heaven.

"I thought you weren't supposed to be able to see Angels," said Dad.

"Well, I can," said Sarah.

"That's because you're very special," said Mum, giving her a hug.

"Maeve can't see Angels!" said Sarah.

"Not yet," said Mum.

They went to church, and had Christmas dinner and then Mum said she wasn't doing any more work and Dad and Sarah did the dishes and Maeve had her sleep and Sarah went out on the skates wearing her crash helmet and Maeve ate her sweets and Sarah's sweets and was sick and then Maeve went to bed and when Maeve was asleep Sarah went to bed.

"Fred didn't come at *all*!" Sarah complained, when Mum was tucking her up. "He promised he would come to see me on Christmas Day, and he didn't, and I kept some chocolate money for his present!"

"I expect your Angel was kept busy," said Mum. "Christmas must be an Extra-Special Day in Heaven."

"He said he would come to see me!" Sarah objected.

"Tell you what," said Mum. "We'll both say a little prayer to make Fred come."

"Yes!" said Sarah.

That's what they did.

"Night-night, Sarah!" said Mum, switching off the light.

Sarah lay very still, counting sheep, waiting for Fred to come zooming down on his cloud.

Then, just as she was about to go to sleep, something happened.

The bedroom lit up with a soft, glowing blue light that spread from the end of Sarah's bed right into the shadows, and made baby Maeve stir in her sleep. Then, there was the sound of gently beating wings, and Fred appeared, on the end of the bed.

"Merry Christmas, Sarah!" Fred said.

"Oh! Oh, Fred! You do look lovely!" said Sarah, and he did.

His robes were gleaming white, and there was a golden light around his head.

"Is that ... is that..."

"My Halo," said Fred proudly. "I'm a proper Angel now. I was made one in the Birthday Honours List!"

"Fred!" said Sarah. "Congratulations!"

Then Fred told her all about Christmas in Heaven, and some of the presents he had been given by the other angels. There was a pair of woolly underpants for night flying, a book on singing for angels (because his singing was still not *quite* right), a 21-week Harping for Beginners course, complete with spare strings, an Angel Recliner for cloud-sitting and a halo-sparkling kit.

"I got you a present, Fred," said Sarah, and she gave him the chocolate money from her stocking, which she had saved for him. It had got a bit squashy, under her pillow, but Fred said it was delicious.

"I have something special for you, too!" said Fred, and he gave her a large slice of the most gorgeous-looking cake she had ever seen, glittering with decorations, and filled up with peaches and cream and strawberries and cherries and bananas and pineapple and nuts and everything lovely in the world, or elsewhere.

"Oh, thank you very much, Fred!" said Sarah, because it looked scrumptious.

"It is my slice of *The* Birthday Cake," said Fred. "I saved it specially for you, Sarah!"

"Whose Birthday?" asked Sarah.

"You know!" said Fred.

"Oh," said Sarah. *"Christmas!"*

"The Most Special Birthday Cake There Is!" said Fred proudly, and Sarah shared her slice with him, and they were both very happy.

A Happy Christmas for the Ghost

by MARTIN WADDELL
illustrated by TONY ROSS

It was Christmas Eve, and the Ghost was busy decorating the coal shed. He had strung red and yellow streamers round the walls, and poked holly through the holes in the tin roof. A piece of mistletoe dangled in the doorway and the Ghost's picture of Florence Nightingale was draped in silver tinsel. In the far corner there glowed a ghostly Christmas tree, all red and green and gold and shiny.

"Oooooooooooh! Ghost!" said Bertie, looking at it with saucer eyes. He thought it was the best Christmas tree he had ever seen.

The Ghost sat down rather unsteadily on the slack, resting his glass on the coal-bucket beside him. The Ghost had just come back from the Spectre's Arms, where he had been having a small extra Festive Haunt, with breaks for refreshments.

"It is time you were in bed, Bertie," said the Ghost. "Santa Claus will soon be here."

"Max says that there is no Santa Claus," said Bertie.

"Max says there are no ghosts," said the Ghost. "But Max doesn't know everything, does he? Ghosts are rather like Santa Claus."

"Are they?" said Bertie.

"Oh yes, they are," said the Ghost. "I'm a ghost, and you believe in me, so you can see me. Max doesn't believe in me, and he can't see me. It is the same with Santa Claus, but more important, because if nobody believed in Santa Claus, there would be no Christmas. I feel sorry for Max."

"So do I," said Bertie, and he went off upstairs to bed.

"Mum," said Bertie, as Mrs Boggin was tucking him in. "Mum, I'm sorry for Max, because Max doesn't believe in Santa Claus."

"Doesn't he?" said Mrs Boggin.

"Mum," said Bertie. "Do *you* believe in Santa Claus?"

"Of course I do, wee Bertie," said Mrs Boggin. "You wait until the morning, and you'll see."

"But you don't believe in ghosts, do you?" said Bertie. "You don't believe in *my* Ghost."

Mrs Boggin took a long time replying. "I don't know, Bertie," she said, in the end. "I don't know what to think about your Ghost. Sometimes I ... but it doesn't really matter what I believe, does it? So long as *you* believe in him."

"That's right," said Bertie. "My Ghost will still be there, so long as I believe in him." And he cuddled down beneath the sheets to go to sleep.

But he didn't go to sleep.

Bertie lay in bed hoping and hoping for a red and yellow tricycle like the one in Mrs Boggin's big catalogue.

"Tricycles cost a lot of money, Bertie," Mrs

Boggin had told him. "But we'll see at Christmas time."

Now it was Christmas, almost.

"TRICYCLE.

"TRICYCLE."

Bertie concentrated very hard, in the hope that believing in tricycles would make one come.

The Ghost came floating into the room and perched on the end of Bertie's bed. He waved at Bertie.

"Just doing my rounds," he said. "I've got to make sure all the stockings are up."

"Mine is one of Dad's," said Bertie, who had picked the biggest sock he could find. Then he asked the Ghost a question.

"Ghost," Bertie said, "if Max doesn't believe in Santa Claus, what will happen to *his* Christmas stocking? You said that there would be no Christmas if people didn't believe in Santa Claus, and Max doesn't."

The Ghost looked serious. "Then you'll have to do his believing for him, Bertie," he said.

"Oh," said Bertie. "Do you think I could?"

"I'm sure you could," said the Ghost.

"I believe in Santa Claus," said Bertie.

"Oh, I know you do," said the Ghost. "Good

night, Bertie," and he glided off in the general direction of the Spectre's Arms and the Haunted Cellar Disco, where his presence was urgently required.

"Tricycle," thought Bertie, thinking very hard, and "I believe in Santa Claus for me *and* Max," and "TRICYCLE," again, and again, and again, because the tricycle was very important.

"TRICYCLE!!!"

He went to sleep.

"Hip-yip hurrah! It's Christmas!" Max was dancing on the stairs. In one hand he waved a telescope, and in the other his half-empty Christmas stocking. He was eating mandarin oranges and chocolate at the same time, with a spud gun sticking out of the belt of his pyjamas.

Elsie said, "Oooooh!" and "Aaaaaah!" and started eating too, whilst she sorted out the lovely things in her stocking. There was a blue scarf and a diary and a pen and a talking doll.

"Toooole-uuuu! Ouuutle-oooo!" went Bertie, on the gold trumpet he had pulled from his stocking. "Tooole-utttle-uttttttle!"

"Children, it is only six o'clock," muttered a bleary-eyed Mr Boggin.

"Hip-yip! Ooooooo-aaah! Toootle-uuttttle-uttle!" went all the Bogginses in chorus, as they headed down the stairs.

The door of the Christmas Room was shut.

The Ghost bounced up and down on the hall-stand, wearing his haunting hat and his pyjamas and eating chocolate doubloons from his stocking. "Wait till you *see*! Wait till you *see* what's in there, Bertie!" he whispered.

"Now," said Mrs Boggin, opening the door of the Christmas Room. "One child at a time. Bertie first, because he is the smallest."

Bertie went into the Christmas Room.

The curtains were pulled tight, the pile of presents was lit by the glint of the Christmas tree lights.

There were fat parcels and thin parcels, big parcels and little parcels and tiny parcels, and green parcels and red parcels and gold parcels and yellow parcels, and parcels that looked like bottles and parcels that didn't, and a thing like a swing ball for Max and a *huge* painting-set for Elsie (complete with easel) and ...

... glittering in the darkness ...

... red and yellow, with a shiny bright bell...

"Tricycle," breathed Bertie. "My TRICYCLE!"

He touched it.

He rang the bell.

It was *real*.

It *really* was.

Everyone had a very happy Christmas at Number 12 Livermore Street.

"You only got that telescope from Santa Claus because of me," Bertie told Max, and Max didn't even thump him.

"You've all eaten too much!" said Mrs Boggin.

"Good," said Mr Boggin, and the rest of the Bogginses agreed with him. All except Tojo, that is, for he was still too busily engaged in eating the biggest-bone-in-the-world (given to him by Max, and tied up with a blue ribbon by Elsie) to agree with anything.

"Time for bed," said Mrs Boggin, at last.

They went to bed.

"Mum," said Bertie, as she was tucking him in, "the Ghost said I was to thank you very much for having him."

"You can tell him it's a pleasure, Bertie," said Mrs Boggin. And then she added, "If I see him, I'll tell him so myself."

"You can't see him, Mum," said Bertie. "You can't see the Ghost if you don't believe in him."

"Y-e-s," said Mrs Boggin. "Well ... you see ... Bertie, I think I—"

"Mum," said Max. "I think I've got a sick tummy."

Mrs Boggin went to deal with Max's tummy. Then she had to rush downstairs to fetch Bertie's book about spiders, which Aunt Amanda had sent him from Ballynahinch. Elsie couldn't sleep, and wanted to get up and watch the late film. Then Mr Boggin couldn't find his slippers.

Mrs Boggin was run off her feet looking after them all.

"Bed," said Mr Boggin, who had had a very hard day sitting down.

Mrs Boggin let Tojo out and in again, stoked up the boiler, put out the kitchen light, stole a nip of cold ham and turkey, and went into the Christmas Room. And there ...

... shimmering in the glow of the Christmas tree lights ...

... fast asleep in the best armchair with a large glass of Mr Boggin's Bristol Cream sherry in his hand ...

... Mrs Boggin *saw* the Ghost.

She stood absolutely still, and her mouth
dropped open.

"Bertie's Ghost!" she gasped.

She didn't waken him. Instead, she put out the light and tiptoed gently out of the room.

Christmas Day in Crocus Street

by DIANA HENDRY
illustrated by JULIE DOUGLAS

It was Christmas Eve. Two families lived in the flats at Crocus Street, and everyone in those two families had a different idea of what they wanted to do on Christmas Day.

Miranda-Gran said that when she had eaten her Christmas dinner she wanted to put up her feet and fall asleep by the fire and *no one* was to say the word "ironing" to her!

Mrs Larkin said that *The Sound of Music* was on television and that she watched it every year and she would like to do so again.

"Christmas time is all stress!" said Sam, lying down on the sofa. "I shall stay cool."

"You better miss Christmas dinner, then," said Mrs Larkin. "It might be too stressful for you."

But Sam sat up at this and said he thought he could just about cope with Christmas dinner.

Mr and Mrs Salkey said they were going to church in the morning and then they were going to walk up Crocus Street and show Winston all the lights on the Christmas trees because this was Winston's very first Christmas.

Lily and Shanta said they were going to play with the toys that Father Christmas brought them. All day!

"What about Christmas dinner?" asked Miranda-Gran. "Mrs Salkey is going to cook us a special Jamaican Christmas dinner." Lily and Shanta said they would stop for that.

But Miranda-Gran didn't get her afternoon sleep by the fire, and Mrs Larkin didn't watch *The Sound of Music* and Shanta and Lily didn't play with their Christmas presents all day and Sam "stayed cool", but it wasn't quite the sort of "cool" he had in mind.

This is what happened.

When Shanta woke up on Christmas Day morning, her room seemed to be lit by a strange white light. Shanta saw that the sock she'd left out for Father Christmas was now bulging nicely and she sat up and reached down to the bottom of the bed for it. As she did so, she glanced out of the window. What she saw gave her an awful fright!

Clutching her Christmas sock, Shanta ran into her parents' bedroom. "There's something wrong with my eyes!" cried Shanta, jumping onto the bed and hiding her face in the eiderdown. "Everything's gone white! All the colours have gone out of the world!"

Mr Salkey sat up in bed, reached for his orange velvet cap and looked out of the window.

"Honey-bee," said Mr Salkey, "what colour is my cap?"

Shanta lifted her face out of the eiderdown and said, "Orange!"

"There's nothing wrong with those eyes of yours," said her dad. "You just haven't seen English snow before."

Then Mrs Salkey got out of bed and took Shanta to the window.

"It's like the icing sugar of the sky!" said Mrs Salkey. "It's like crumbs of fresh bread!"

Shanta looked even more surprised. "Icing sugar? Breadcrumbs? Can you eat that snow-stuff?"

"No," said Mrs Salkey, "but you can have a whole snowball-full of fun with it!"

All morning it snowed and it snowed and it snowed. A few cars slithered up and down Crocus Street. Lily and Sam's dad came to call with snow on his hat and snow on his shoes and snow on the Christmas parcels he'd brought for them.

Mr and Mrs Salkey went to church in a flaky snowstorm and they showed Winston the Christmas tree lights. When they came in they said, "It's getting very deep."

Shanta and Lily played with their Christmas presents and every so often they ran to the window to see how the snow was doing.

"Spoons and scoops of icing sugar!" said Shanta.

"Loaves and loaves of breadcrumbs!" said Lily.

From upstairs in the Salkeys' flat came wonderful warm smells and after a while Mr Salkey appeared at the top of the stairs with a sprig of holly in his cap and said, "Christmas dinner is ready for all you good people."

They had pumpkin soup and then Mrs Salkey brought in a great bowl of her special Jamaican dish.

"It's got all sorts of surprises in it," said Lily when she was given her plate. And it had. There were black-eyed beans and spicy chicken pieces. There were slivers of fish hiding in the rice. There were okra pods and carrots and slices of fried bananas.

"Brill!" said Sam.

"Yummy!" said Mrs Larkin.

"Happy Christmas!" said Miranda-Gran.

After the Christmas pudding (with Jamaican rum for the grown-ups) and after the crackers and hats (which Mrs Larkin had brought) and when all the dishes were done, they looked out of the window at Crocus Street covered in snow. They saw lots of families walking down the street, carrying trays. A few people had wooden boxes with a rope fixed like a handle at one end.

"Where are they all going?" asked Lily, "and why are they taking their trays?"

"I know," said Miranda-Gran. "They're going sledging in the park."

"Can we go? Can we go? Can we go?" Shanta and Lily cried at once.

And Sam said, "Yes. Sledging is cool."

"Particularly on the bottom," said Miranda-Gran.

Then all the grown-ups looked at each other and Mrs Larkin said, "I've got a tray that would make a very good sledge," and Mr Salkey said, "We've got a fruit box. I could easily make a handle for it."

And very soon they all had their hats and coats and scarves and gloves and boots on and they were out in Crocus Street with all the other families, heading for the park.

It was very nice being out in the street. Everyone called out, "Happy Christmas!" and Lily and Shanta saw lots of their friends from school. Everyone was wearing bright woolly hats and scarves and gloves. They were as brightly wrapped up as Christmas parcels!

The park was very good for sledging because it had low slopes and high slopes. Sam used the tray because he was old enough to go down the big slope by himself. Mr Salkey put Shanta and Lily together on the wooden box-sledge and pulled them down it. After a while they could both go by themselves, but first Lily, then Shanta, fell off into the snow.

"You're both snowy-glowy!" said Miranda-Gran after about an hour. And it was true. Lily's mittens dripped with snow but her cheeks glowed like apples.

Then Mr Salkey sat on the box-sledge and held Winston in his arms and went down the small

slope very, very gently. Winston waved his arms in the air and crowed with pleasure. He tried to eat some snow but it was so cold he spat it out again.

Everything in the park looked very different covered in snow. The roundabout vanished under it. The swings each had a little cushion of snow on their seats and all the branches of the trees were topped with a finger of icing sugar.

Sam and Mr Salkey showed Lily and Shanta how to make snowballs and then they had a snowball fight and got very wet indeed.

Soon it grew dark and everyone left the park tired but happy. Lily and Shanta were so tired that Mr Salkey said he would pull them home on the sledge. Mrs Salkey carried Winston on her back and he fell fast asleep.

When they had hung all their wet clothes up to dry and Mrs Larkin had lit the fire and drawn the curtains, Miranda-Gran made some hot chocolate. "It's too late for my afternoon nap," she said.

"And it's too late for *The Sound of Music*," said Mrs Larkin.

"Well, now," said Mr Salkey, "I suppose we better have a game of something. I don't suppose Father Christmas brought you girls any games we could play, did he?"

"He did! He did!" cried Lily and Shanta and they rushed off to fetch them. Lily had Ludo and Shanta had Snakes and Ladders and there was just time for one game of each.

"Do you know what was my best present?" Shanta asked Lily at bedtime.

"No. What?" asked Lily.

"Snow!" said Shanta.

And that was Christmas Day in Crocus Street.

King
of Kings

by SUSAN HILL
illustrated by JOHN LAWRENCE

Mr Hegarty hadn't always been alone. And being alone didn't always mean being lonely. But quite often it did.

Once, there had been Mrs Hegarty, whose name had been Doll, or sometimes Dolly, and they had been married for a great many years, and there had been good days and bad days but mostly good, some ups and some downs, but mostly ups, and the great many years had not seemed nearly enough before Mrs Hegarty got ill and then very much iller, and died. So that now there was only Mr Hegarty and Cat the cat, and Jacko.

Cat the cat had never been bought or in any other way chosen, he had just come – one day onto the wall, the next day in the yard, the third day into the house, and after that, as Mr Hegarty said, paws under the table for good.

Cat, like all cats, came and went as he pleased. But Jacko had been chosen all right, for his black-patch eye and his brave, bright bark, and for being cheap from the man with the barrow in the lane, because his legs were bandy.

Mr Hegarty's house was the last in the street. After it came the wharves and warehouses, the waste ground and the church, the building site, the road and the railway.

But walk another way and there were still a few streets left. Though not the street where Mr Hegarty was born and grew to be a man, nor the one where Mrs Hegarty had been born and got married from, all those years ago. They are gone, and their neighbours' houses too, and the pub and the shop on the corner, pulled down in heaps of dust and rubble and carted away on skips and lorries.

There were cranes now, and site offices, concrete girders and craters in the ground, men in hard hats and machines, judder-judder, all day, all day.

But walk a bit further still, which Mr Hegarty and Jacko always did, and there was the Lane, just as it had always been, and the streets and squares around it, and shops and buses and flats and people, schools and churches, the bit of park and the King's Hospital.

And now it was Christmas Eve. Mr Hegarty had been about all day. He liked to be about. He liked Christmas Eve. Everybody talked to everybody else and there was a lot of bustle; people were cheerful. He'd been about the market, among the stalls and barrows. Then, he and Jacko had stood for a long time on the corner, just for the pleasure of watching everything. He'd had his dinner out – pie and chips – and his tea, with a mince pie "on the house". Lotta, who kept the café, had said, "because ees Christmas".

But now it was late. Dark. Now, everything was

closing down. They were sweeping up around the barrows, sprigs of holly and paper from the oranges and a few lost sprouts.

"Goodnight, then. Happy Christmas."

Lamps out. Blinds up. Shutters down.

The main road was jammed. The trains went along the line, full of everyone going home. So Mr Hegarty and Jacko went home too. Across the building site. Quiet now, the great crane still and silent. It had a Christmas tree balanced on the very end, with lights and decorations. But the men had finished at dinner time today.

Past the warehouses and wharves. Once, Mr Hegarty had been a nightwatchman on the wharf. That was when the ships had docked, years ago. There were no ships now.

Across the last bit of waste ground. Jacko's ears twitched.

Home.

Christmas Eve. The wind blew down alleyways, across the dark wharves, smelling of rain and river. No snow. No star. But Christmas Eve isn't often like the stories.

Mr Hegarty reached home. There was a carrier bag on the step, with three wrapped-up presents inside, and a card. "To Mr Hegarty and Jacko and

Cat, a Happy Christmas, with love from Jo."

Jo and his family lived next door. But they had gone away that morning, to stay with his grandmother for the holiday. One day, they'd go away altogether. Everybody would. This was the last street. Mr Hegarty didn't want to think about it.

Nothing inside the house had changed very much since he and Mrs Hegarty moved in, newly married; and since Mrs Hegarty died, nothing had changed at all. Mr Hegarty wanted it like that, just as it was and had always been and as she had left it.

He kept it clean and put things away in the same old places and polished the windows and blackened the hearth and washed up in the stone sink and slept in the big brass bed.

And every Christmas, he put up the decorations, around the pictures and over the mirror and along the mantelpiece, with a wreath of holly on the front door, just as Mrs Hegarty always had.

It was very quiet. Mr Hegarty went into the scullery to wash his hands, then fed Jacko and Cat, put the kettle on, made up the fire and sat beside it. And Mrs Hegarty sat beside him, smiling out from the silver photograph frame on the little table.

Later, the band came and played "Silent Night" and "Hark, the Herald Angels" under the orange lamp at the end of the street, and the man with the collecting tin came down to Mr Hegarty's door and they had a chat. Then, they played one more carol, which was "In the Bleak Mid-winter", because it had been Mrs Hegarty's favourite, before they went away. But for quite a while, the strains of trumpet and tuba and cornet, "O Little Town of Bethlehem" and "While Shepherds Watched" floated faintly back to him across the wharves and waste ground. Then, it was quiet again.

For the rest of the evening, while Jacko and Cat slept on the hearth rug, Mr Hegarty sat in his armchair, thinking, as people do, of other Christmases, good and bad and in between – but mostly good, for times past are golden in the memory to an old and lonely man.

At ten o'clock, he got up, and Jacko ran to the front door, and they went for their last walk, up the street and down again. There was nobody about, though some of the houses had lights on, glowing behind curtains, and two of them had Christmas trees in the windows.

And the wind still blew, down the alleyways and across the wharves and waste ground, with the

smell of the river on its breath.

Christmas Eve. Mr Hegarty's heart lifted. It was still special, after all, there was no getting away from that. Then, he let Cat out, locked up, wound his watch, and went upstairs to bed.

Some time after midnight, he woke again. At first, he didn't know why. There was no sound, except for Jacko, snoring softly. Then, there was something, a very faint, distant sound, not inside the house, out. Mr Hegarty put on his slippers, went downstairs, and opened the front door.

Everything was still. It had stopped raining and the wind had died down.

The moon shone.

Jacko came pattering down the stairs and stopped beside Mr Hegarty at the front door.

There it was again. Very faint. A mewling sound. Kittens?

Mr Hegarty put on his coat and shoes and took the torch. Then, he went out of the house and across the waste ground, towards the church. Jacko ran ahead, ears cocked, tail up.

There were railings round the old church, but the padlock on the gate was broken. The sound was louder. Mr Hegarty stopped. The moon came out again from behind a cloud. Jacko had trotted up the weed-covered path to the church porch and Mr Hegarty could see him standing beside something, wagging his tail. So he went too.

Here, the sound was loud and clear and unmistakable.

Mr Hegarty shone his torch.

On a ledge inside the dark, damp, cold stone porch of the church stood a shallow cardboard box.

Inside the box lay a baby.

It was very small, and wrapped in a scruffy piece of blanket.

"Now then!" said Mr Hegarty softly. "Now then."

But then he didn't know quite what to do.

He and Mrs Hegarty had never had any children. Mr Hegarty had never even held a baby. In his own home, there had been seven children, but as he had been the youngest, all the others had picked him up.

The moon went behind a cloud again, and the baby stopped crying and just lay. Jacko sat, waiting.

"Well," said Mr Hegarty.

And then, because there was nothing else that he could do, he picked up the box with the baby in it, very gently. And as he did so, he remembered that it was not Christmas Eve any longer, but Christmas Day.

Then, carrying the box very carefully, he

made his way slowly out of the church porch and back across the waste ground, Jacko trotting at his heels. He couldn't hold the torch as well, so he put it at the bottom of the box, by the baby's feet.

Up the street, past the building site and the wharves and warehouses, empty and silent, towards the streets, and then the market, the shops, the Lane. His footsteps echoed.

The pubs and cafés had long since shut. The last trains had gone, and there were no cars on the main road.

Mr Hegarty walked on, stopping now and then to set the box down and rest his arms.

Then Jacko stopped too, and waited patiently.

The baby had gone to sleep.

From across the last square, beside the bit of park, Mr Hegarty could see the lights shining out.

"Now then," he said. But then, just for a minute, he didn't want to go on, didn't want to let the baby go. He felt a strange, half-sad, half-angry feeling, like a knot tightening inside him. Whoever could have left it in a box, in a cold porch, at Christmas? He looked down at it again. But then, because he knew there was only one right thing to do, he crossed the road and walked up the drive to the entrance.

"Stay," he said. Jacko stayed.

Then, Mr Hegarty went through the glass doors into the lighted entrance of the King's Hospital.

In the hall, there was a huge Christmas tree, and paper chains and decorations strung from the ceiling and all around the walls. At the far end was a reception desk, with a porter behind it, and a nurse standing beside. Mr Hegarty went up to them and stood, holding the box in his arms.

"I've brought a baby," he said.

In the next hour or so, a lot of things happened. The baby was taken away, and Mr Hegarty asked to sit down and answer a great many questions, from a nurse, and a doctor and finally, from two policemen. They brought him a cup of tea, and then another, with a pink bun, and asked him to sign some papers, and the whole time, Jacko sat without moving or barking, on the step beyond the glass doors.

But in the end, the nurse came back again and said, "You can go now, Mr Hegarty. You must be tired out."

"Right," said the policemen. "We'll drop you off. Trafalgar Street, isn't it?"

Mr Hegarty stood up. He was tired, tired enough to drop, and muddled and, in a way, sad.

"No, thank you very much," he said. "If it's all the same to you, I'll walk." And he went slowly across the blue carpet to the glass doors, where Jacko was waiting.

"Come on then," Mr Hegarty said. Jacko came.

He did sleep, just a bit, but it was a strange, restless sleep, full of odd dreams and noises.

When he woke properly, it was just coming light. Grey. Damp looking. "Happy Christmas, Jacko," Mr Hegarty said. Jacko hardly stirred.

He was going to make a pot of tea, and then open his present from Jo. But, as he washed, he knew that he wouldn't, not yet. Knew that he would have to go there first, straight away, because the baby had been on his mind all night, and he couldn't settle until he'd made sure about it.

He let Cat in, whistled to Jacko, and crossed the street, all over again, in the same direction as before.

And as he walked, he wondered. Whose baby? When? How? Why? What would happen to it now?

He hadn't even found out what it was, girl or boy, hadn't liked to ask.

The hospital looked different in the early morning light, larger, greyer, somehow less friendly.

But he left Jacko on the step again, and went in, down the blue carpet.

After he had explained, they left him, sitting on a chair in a corridor. The hospital was still quiet, but not like the night before. He could hear doors banging and the lift going up and down. Perhaps they would bring him a cup of tea again. He always had one as soon as he got up. He was missing it now.

But it didn't really matter. He'd had to come.

"Mr Hegarty?"

Mr Hegarty stood up.

"Would you like to come with me?"

Through doors. Down a corridor.

"I'm sure you'd like to see him, wouldn't you?"

Him. A boy then. Yes, that was as it should be.

"He's fine, thanks to you. But if you hadn't found him…"

They went down more corridors. Around corners. Through doors. Stopped.

"You'll see that we've done something special," she said. "We always wait for the first baby born in the hospital on Christmas Day, but there hasn't been one yet. And besides, we thought that your baby was the most important one here today. Come in and see."

There were babies in small cots. Through a glass window, he could see beds.

"Look, Mr Hegarty."

At the end of the room, on a small, raised platform, stood a crib, draped and decorated, under a canopy. Hanging above the canopy was a star. "The Christmas crib," she said. "Only used once a year. Today."

Mr Hegarty went a step closer. Looked down. And there he was, the baby from the cardboard box in the dark church porch, the baby he had found and carried here with Jacko. The Christmas baby.

For a while, Mr Hegarty didn't speak.

Then he said quietly, "King of Kings. That's who he is. The King of Kings." And went, smiling, out of the nursery.

They did find him a cup of tea, and a breakfast too, and a plate of sausages for Jacko, and said they would be letting him know what happened to the baby, when there was any news.

"And you'll be welcome to come and see him you know," the nurse said. "Any day."

"Thank you," Mr Hegarty said. "Thank you very much. I should like that."

And then he went home, with Jacko trotting beside him, through the quiet early streets of Christmas morning.

Acknowledgements

The publisher would like to thank the following
for permission to reproduce their work:

Christmas in Exeter Street
Text © 1989 Diana Hendry   Illustrations © 1989 John Lawrence

"In Which Tom Appears" from *Sophie's Tom*
Text © 1991 Dick King-Smith   Illustrations © 1991 David Parkins

The Haunting of Pip Parker
Text © 1991 Anne Fine   Illustrations © 1992 Emma Chichester Clark

"Caroline's Christmas" from *Caroline Columbus*
Text © 1990 Mick Gowar   Illustrations © 1990 Duncan Smith

The Boot Gang's Christmas Caper
Text © 1988 Sarah Hayes   Illustrations © 1988 Juan Wijngaard

The Christmas Miracle of Jonathan Toomey
Text © 1995 Susan Wojciechowski   Illustrations © 1995 P.J. Lynch

"Sarah's Christmas" from *Fred the Angel*
Text © 1989 Martin Waddell   Illustrations © 1989 Patrick Benson

"A Happy Christmas for the Ghost" from *The Ghost and Bertie Boggin*
Text © 1980, 2000 Martin Waddell   Illustrations © 2000 Tony Ross

"Christmas Day in Crocus Street" from *Flower Street Friends*
Text © 1995 Diana Hendry   Illustrations © 1995 Julie Douglas

King of Kings
Text © 1993 Susan Hill   Illustrations © 1993 John Lawrence

Title page illustration © 1992 Emma Chichester Clark